Animals in my Room

by Alexandra Welch-Zerba

Illustrations by Sheila Welch

Published 2017

Animals in my Room
ISBN-10:
0-692-89922-7
ISBN-13:
978-0-692-89922-9

Published 2017

www.animalsinmyroom.com
(603) 340-8307

The illustrations for this book were rendered using colored pencil.

For Anna,
our inspiration

Wishing every child
the wonders of a magical dream.

Acknowledgements

Special thanks to
my husband, Mark,
for his love and support,
to my sister, Lisa, and
my father, John,
for their continuous encouragement,
to Crystal Ward Kent,
for all of her time, patience and guidance,
and to my mother, Sheila,
for without her dedication and artistic talent,
this book would not have been possible.

The stars are out,
it's time for bed,
I pick up Teddy Bear.
Then walk upstairs
to wash my face,
and brush my teeth with care.

5

I change into my nightgown,
and nestle into bed.
And as I start to fall asleep,
dreams pop into my head.

APPLES FOR PIGS

HONEY FOR BEARS

8

Amazing animals are in my room;
I can't believe my eyes!
Piggy sits upon my dresser,
and Teddy's twice my size!

Miss Kangaroo enjoys a snack,
while Kitty climbs the drapes.
And Pink Flamingo struts about,
with tasty, juicy grapes.

Parrot rests upon my shoulder.
Butterfly lands on my nose.
Puppy is feeling playful now,
as Lizard tickles my toes!

SNACKS
FOR
GOOD
PUPPIES

King Lion stops to say "hello."
Mouse tip-toes everywhere.
And long, white-bearded Billy Goat
is chewing on my hair!

Baby Elephant sits at my feet.
He's chubby and so cute!
Dear Miss Rabbit eats her carrots,
lettuce, beets and fruit.

PEANUTS FOR ELEPHANTS

PEANUTS

Giraffe is looking in the mirror.
Frogs dream of whirling bugs.
Gentle Tiger, with a smile,
is giving me a hug!

Turtle strolls across the floor.
Bee buzzes all around.
Sweet Alligator glides nearby,
to see what Monkey found.

Soon Unicorn comes prancing in,
and takes me for a ride.
While Sheep shows off her brand new hat,
with Squirrel by her side.

24

These lively, friendly pals of mine
are magical and fun.
Will they stay in my room all night
...each and every one?

25

When I wake up in the morning,
as funny as it seems,
My very own stuffed animals
were all just in my dream!

27

I hug my fuzzy, little friends,
so cuddly, soft and small.
Puppy, Tiger, Teddy Bear...
I love them, one and all!

~ The End ~

About the Author:

Alexandra was born on Nantucket Island, Massachusetts, and has always dreamed of writing a children's book. She has never actually seen a live unicorn or alligator in her room, but her daughter has over 100 beloved stuffed animals in hers, including her two favorites, Doggy and Teddy. Alexandra lives in Bow, New Hampshire with her husband, daughter and five cats.

About the Illustrator:

Since Sheila was a very small child, her favorite pastime was to draw. After graduating from the Rhode Island School of Design, she worked for a small art agency in Boston, Massachusetts, and then moved to Nantucket, Massachusetts, where she started her own commercial art business. With retirement came a move to Portsmouth, New Hampshire and time to experiment with watercolors, and design greeting cards for family and friends. Sheila now lives with her husband in Exeter, New Hampshire where she continues to enjoy working with pen, pencil and brush.

Made in the USA
Lexington, KY
05 October 2017